# The GHOST in the ATTIC

Written by Robyn Supraner

Illustrated by Eulala Conner

**Troll Associates**

Troll Associates

Library of Congress Catalog Card Number: 78-18039
ISBN 0-89375-083-2
10  9  8  7  6  5  4  3

# The GHOST in the ATTIC

One morning, when Peter was eating his oatmeal, he heard a funny sound.

"I hear a funny sound," he told his mother.

His mother stopped to listen.

"I don't hear anything," she said. "It must be your imagination."

That afternoon, when he was playing Go Fish with his sister, Peter heard the funny sound again.

"I hear a funny sound," he told his sister.

His sister stopped to listen.
"I don't hear anything," she said. "It's your imagination."

That night, when his father was tucking him into bed, Peter heard the funny sound a third time.

"I hear a funny sound," he told his father.

His father stopped to listen.

"I don't hear anything," he said. "Really,
Peter, what an imagination you have!"

Peter knew it was not his imagination.
So that night, when everyone was asleep, he
got out of bed. He put on his slippers. He
got his flashlight. Then, he tiptoed out of
his room.

Slowly, step by step, Peter crept down
the long, dark hall.

There! Peter heard it again. The funny
sound was coming from the attic.

*ooooooooooooh whooooooooooo hooooooo*

Peter stopped. The hair on his neck felt strange. He thought of turning back. But he didn't.

Down the hall and up the stairs he went. When he got to the attic door, he listened. He heard a rush. He heard a shush. He heard a whush.

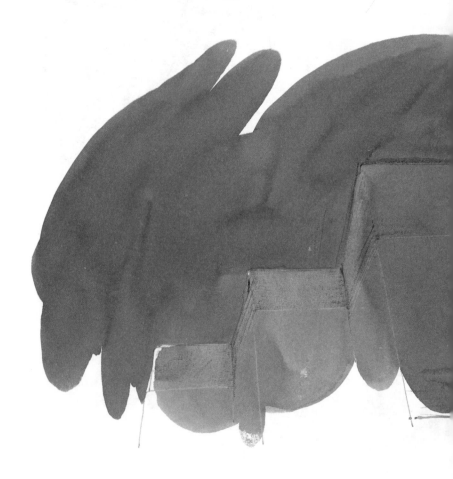

Then, he opened the door and stepped
into the darkness.

Lumpy shadows filled the room. Peter shined his light on them. He saw piles of boxes and dusty books. He saw the crib that used to be his, when he was little. He saw an old bird cage and a tall chest of drawers.

*What was that!* Someone was hiding in the corner! Someone tall! Someone terrible! Someone with a head as big as a pumpkin!

Peter's hands shook. His knees shook. His teeth chattered.

He stepped closer. Closer. Closer. Now he was so close, he could almost reach out and touch the monster in the corner!

Whew! It was only the dummy his mother used for her sewing. On its shoulders, staring out of hollow eyes, sat an old jack-o'-lantern.

Peter's flashlight moved on. Behind its yellow beam, the shadows danced like wavy ghosts.

"Pooh!" said Peter. "Who believes in ghosts?"

"I do," said a small voice from the
corner of the room.

"Wh-wh-who's th-th-there?" asked
Peter. There was no answer.

"Wh-wh-who is i-i-it?" he asked again.
But again, there was no answer.

Peter shined his light into a corner. Something moved. Something small and white. Then it was gone. He heard another rush. And a shush. And a whush.

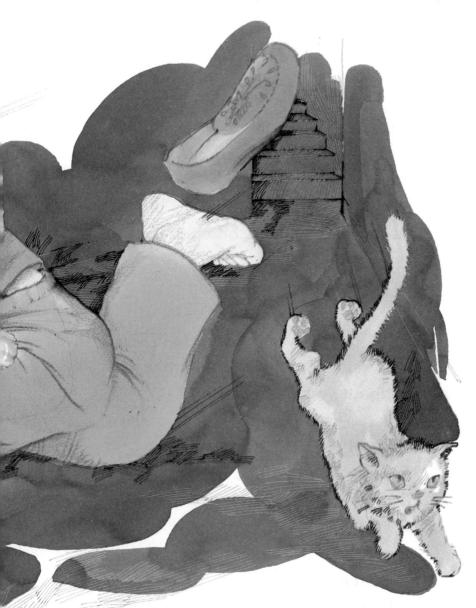

Peter didn't wait to find out what it was.
He went back to his room. He ran all the
way.

The next morning, one of his slippers was missing. He looked everywhere, but it was gone.

Later, when he was eating his breakfast, Peter said, "There is someone hiding in the attic."

"Of course there isn't," said his mother.

"Tell me another," said his sister.

"Don't be silly," said his father. "And Peter," he said frowning, "remember what we said about your imagination."

"But . . . " said Peter.

His mother said, "No buts!"

"But . . . " said Peter.

His father said, "You heard your mother!"

"But . . . " said Peter.

His sister giggled.

So Peter finished his breakfast. He didn't say another word.

At ten o'clock, Peter's mother was missing a saucepan. "Now, where is that saucepan?" she wondered.

At two o'clock, Peter's brother tripped over a skate that somebody left on the stairs. "Who left that dumb skate there, anyway?" he asked. Nobody knew.

At six o'clock, Peter's father looked
everywhere, but could not find his favorite
pipe. "WHO TOOK MY PIPE?"
he thundered. Nobody knew.

Peter said nothing. Not a word.

Late that night, he went back to the attic. Softly, softly, he opened the door.

The moonlight was shining through the window. In its silver light, Peter saw something. It was standing on a washtub in front of a tall mirror. It was making scary faces. It was making funny sounds.

*ooooooooh whoooooooooo hooooooooooooooooo*

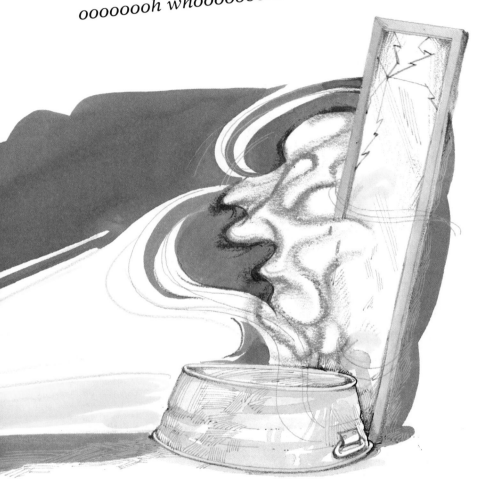

Peter turned on his flashlight. The thing
jumped into the air. It started to run away.
"Stop!" cried Peter. The thing stopped.

"Wh-wh-who are y-y-y-you?" asked Peter.

"I am Pipchick, the ghostling," said a very little ghost.

"Pipchick?" said Peter. "What kind of a name is that?"

"A terrible name," said Pipchick. He moaned, a long, sad moan. "Alas, I am but a ghostling ... "

"Alas?" said Peter.

"That's ghost talk," said Pipchick.

"Oh," said Peter. "I didn't know."

"Alas," said Pipchick again. "I am but a ghostling. But someday, when I am truly a real ghost, I will be called Pip."

"What are you doing in my attic?" asked Peter.

"Questions, questions, questions," grumbled Pipchick. "Well, if you really must know, I'm doing my homework."

"Your homework?" said Peter.

"There you go again," said the ghostling. "Do you always ask so many questions?" He handed a piece of paper to Peter. There was writing on it. It said: 619 Berry Street.

"That's my address!" cried Peter.

"Of course," said the ghostling. "That's why I'm here. I have to do my homework in a home, don't I? This is only my practice home. I have to practice scaring people and hiding things. When I get good enough, I'm going to have my very own castle to haunt!"

"Aha!" said Peter. "I bet you were the one who took my mother's saucepan and my father's pipe! I bet you were the one who left the skate on the stairs and hid my slipper! Right? Am I right?"

"Absolutely!" said Pipchick.

Then he showed Peter his secret hiding place. "Look," he said, with just a touch of pride.

Peter looked. He saw a red crayon he
thought was lost. He saw a skate key and
two mittens that didn't match. He saw his
mother's saucepan and his father's pipe. He
saw his missing slipper and an old yellow
rain hat. And lots more.

"I'd like my slipper back, if you don't mind," said Peter.

"Of course," said Pipchick. He handed the slipper to Peter. "Well?" he asked. He stood back and admired his work. "How am I doing?"

"To tell the truth," said Peter, "You're pretty good at hiding things, but not so good at scaring. I'm the only one who can hear you. You have to speak louder. You should learn to speak up more."

"Is that so?" said the ghostling. "I'd appreciate it very much if you'd show me what you mean."

"Well," said Peter. "For one thing, your
*hooooo* is too soft. Try it like this." Peter
cupped his hands around his mouth.
"*HOOOOOOOOOOOOO*," he called, as loudly
as he could.

"Like this?" asked Pipchick. He flapped his sheet and took a deep breath.

"*HOOOOooooooooo?*"

"No," said Peter. "The ending is no good. You have to keep it loud. Stand up straight and open your mouth. Like this—

*HOOOOOOOOOOOOOOOO!*"

"I think I've got it," said Pipchick. He threw back his head and opened his mouth as wide as he could. He flapped his sheet and flew around the room. Out came the scariest sound that Peter had ever heard.

"*WHOOOOOooooOOOOOOOOOoooooo.*"

"Perfect!" said Peter. "That's really scary! I'll have to call you Pip from now on." Pip grinned proudly.

Suddenly, from downstairs, Peter's
sister called: "HELLLLLLLLP! THERE'S A
GHOST IN THE HOUSE!"

Then they heard Peter's mother and father. "There, there," said his mother. "It was only a dream." "Go back to sleep," said his father. "It was nothing at all."

"I'd better go now," said Peter. "We woke up the whole family! But first, I want you to promise to put everything back where you found it."

"Do I have to?" asked Pipchick.

"Of course," said Peter. "You're not a ghostling anymore."

"That's true," said Pip. "Everything will be back by morning. I have to go, too. My work is finished here."

"I'll miss you," said Peter. "Goodbye, Pip."

"Goodbye, Peter. I'll miss you, too." Then, right before Peter's eyes, the little ghost flew into the air and disappeared into the shadows.

The next morning, everything was back in its place.

"What do you know," said Peter's mother when she came into the kitchen. "My saucepan was in the cupboard all the time. Funny I didn't see it."

"I can't understand it," said Peter's

father. "My pipe is right here, where it belongs. Why didn't I see it last night?"

"Look at this," said Peter's sister. "My old skate key. I thought I lost it long ago. What's it doing here?"

They all looked at Peter. There was a twinkle in his eye.

"Peter," said his father, "do you know
anything about all this?"

Peter looked at his father. He looked at
his mother. He looked at his sister.

"Whooo, me?" he said.

Then he finished his breakfast. He didn't
say another word. Not a word.